Maisy Goes to a Show

Lucy Cousins

WALKER BOOKS
AND SUBSIDIARIES

LONDON · BOSTON · SYDNEY · AUCKLAND

Today, Maisy and her friends are going to the theatre.

The show is called "Funny Feathers" and the star is Flora Fantastica.

Inside, everyone queues to show their tickets.
Maisy is **VERY** excited.

"Tickets please!"

Maisy picks up a special book all about the show. It has lovely pictures in it.

They walk into the main theatre and find their seats. Here they are!

Maisy and her friends are in the very front row!

Everyone sits down as the music starts playing. The show is about to begin!

"Shhh!" says Eddie.

The audience is very quiet as the curtain goes up...

Flora flies on to the stage!

"Hello, everyone!" she says.
"Shout 'Funny Feathers!' if
   you're excited about the show!"

"Funny Feathers!" everyone
shouts. Tallulah is the loudest!

In the play, Flora lives in the jungle. She dreams of being a star in the big city!

"I'll come with you!" says Barry Baboon.

Chula and Pedro join in.
"Cock-a-doodle-doo!"
"Let's go too!"

"Follow me –
I know the way!"
calls Larry Lion.

Between the scenes, special helpers
come out onto the stage.

They roll the jungle trees away.
Here comes the big city!

Flora sings a
funny song,
then the curtain
comes down!

It's time for
the interval.
Maisy and Cyril
go to the loo.

Charley buys lots of yummy snacks to share.

Soon a bell rings. Ding Dong! "Time to go back to our seats," says Eddie.

The curtain rises, and the show starts again. Everyone is having fun singing in the big city.

"We love fluffy, funny feathers!"

After some adventures in the city, Flora and her friends decide to go home to their beautiful jungle.

The show ends with a singalong song, and then the actors wave goodbye.

Everyone cheers very loudly.

"Woohoo!"

"Bravo!"   "Hooray!"

They all stand up and clap, and
then it is time to go home.

Clap! Clap!

Clap!

Maisy and her friends walk home together.
They're still singing the songs from the show!
What a lovely trip to the theatre!

"We love fluffy, funny feathers!"

"Doo-de-doo-doo."